THE
PRINCE
AND
THE
PEE

Greg Gormley

illustrated by

Chris Mould

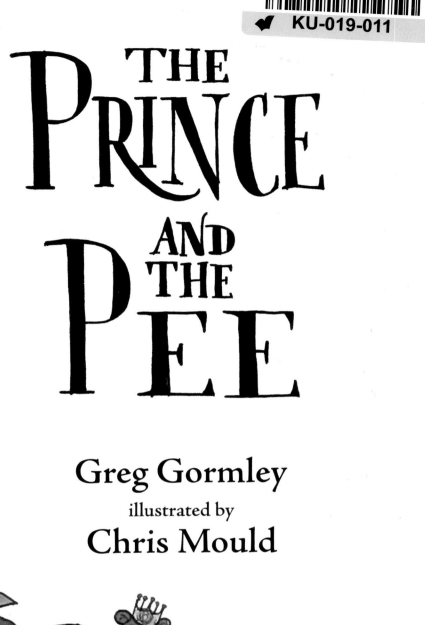

nosy crow

Prince Freddie was on holiday.

He was sunbathing outside the royal tent,
reading comics and slurping the lemoniest
lemonade he had ever tasted.

When suddenly . . .

. . . his horse, Sir Rushington, appeared.

"Your Royal Highness," said the horse,
"a terrible dragon is attacking Castle Crumbly!
We must go and save everyone!"

"Righty-ho!"
said Prince Freddie.

He gulped down
the very last drop of his lemonade,
then he jumped onto Sir Rushington
and they galloped away.

They hadn't gone very far when Prince Freddie felt a tingling.
"I need to pee," he said.

Sir Rushington sighed. "Your Royal Highness,
you should have gone before we left."

"I didn't need to go then," said the prince.

Up and **down** bobbed Prince Freddie
as his horse clip-clopped along.

Up and **down.**

Up and **down.**

Up and **down.**

"Ooh," said the prince. "I need to pee."

"Try to think of something else,"
said Sir Rushington,

"something . . . dry."

So Prince Freddie thought
about sunshine, dusty deserts and
anything at all apart from water.

Just then, it started to rain.
**Plink, plink,
plinkety plink.**

It rattled down on
Prince Freddie's armour.

"I really **need** to pee,"
said Prince Freddie,
"or I'm going to wet my
metal pants."

"Well, don't pee in that armour,
Your Royal Highness,"
said Sir Rushington.
"You'll get all rusty.
I'll stop. But be **quick**."

Prince Freddie jumped down
and clattered over to
a large boulder.

But before Prince Freddie could even unbuckle his armour,
a great big ugly ogre jumped out.

"BOO!"

it shouted.

Prince Freddie almost leapt out
of his iron socks.
"Yikes!" he yelled.

He jumped back
onto Sir Rushington
and galloped away.

"Better?" asked Sir Rushington.
"No," said Prince Freddie. "I couldn't go.
There was an **ogre.**"

"An ogre?" said Sir Rushington.
"How very alarming."

Up and **down** bobbed
Prince Freddie as his horse
clip-clopped along.

Up and **down.**
Up and **down.**
Up and **down.**

"Ooh, I really, **really** need to pee!" said Prince Freddie.

"Very well, Your Royal Highness," said Sir Rushington. "Maybe you could pee behind that tower over there?"

"Perfect!" said Prince Freddie.

But before Prince Freddie
could even undo his metal
trousers, a beautiful princess
stuck her head out of
the window.

"You took
your time!"

she shouted down.

"Have you come
to rescue me?"

"No!" shouted back Prince Freddie.
"I mean, yes, of course.
Just not right now . . .
I'll be back later."

And he jumped back onto
Sir Rushington and
galloped away.

"Better?" asked Sir Rushington.

"No," said Prince Freddie. "I couldn't go. There was a **princess**."

"A princess?" said Sir Rushington. "How very awkward."

Up and **down** bobbed Prince Freddie
as his horse clip-clopped along.

Up and **down**.
　　Up and **down**.
　　　　Up and **down**.

"Look, I'm sorry,
but I really,
really,
really need to pee,"

said Prince Freddie.

"If you must, Your Royal Highness,"
said Sir Rushington.
"There's a forest over there.
But do be **quick.**"

Prince Freddie rushed to the first tree he could see, but the forest was busy.

"Hey, it's my turn to pee," growled the Big Bad Wolf.

"I'm next," miaowed
Puss in Boots.

"And we're after him!"
said the Seven Dwarfs.

"Aaargh! I can't wait that long," said poor Prince Freddie.
He jumped back onto Sir Rushington and galloped away.

"Better?" asked Sir Rushington.

"No," said Prince Freddie. "I couldn't go.
There was a terribly long **queue.**"

"A queue?" said Sir Rushington. "How very tiresome.
But no more stops, Your Royal Highness.
We have a castle to save."

They hadn't gone very far when Prince Freddie asked,
"Are we nearly there yet?"

"Not yet, Your Royal Highness,"
said Sir Rushington.

Five minutes went by.

"Are we nearly there yet?"
asked Prince Freddie.

"No," said Sir Rushington.

After two more minutes
Prince Freddie said,

"Are we nearly there yet?
I'm desperate!"

"Yes, Your Royal Highness, we're here," said Sir Rushington. "There's the . . .

. . . dragon!"

Right in front of the castle gates stood the biggest, fiercest dragon that Prince Freddie had ever seen.

"What do you want, little tin man?" she asked.

"I want . . ." said Prince Freddie, crossing his legs.

"Come on, spit it out," said the dragon.

"I want . . ." said Prince Freddie, hopping up and down.

"**What?**" shouted the dragon.

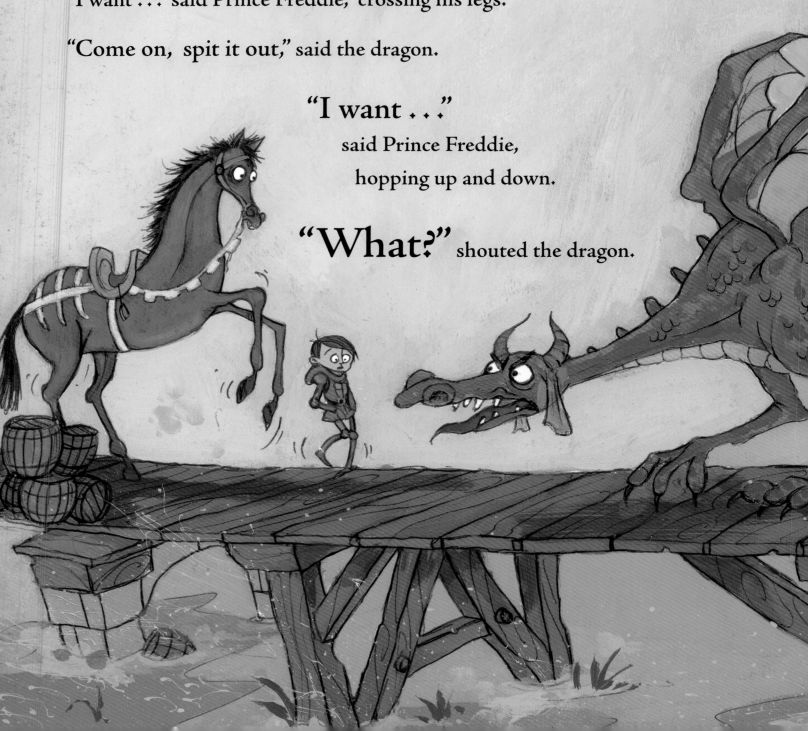

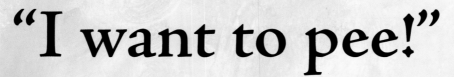

"I want to pee!"

cried Prince Freddie and charged straight at the dragon,
who was so shocked that she jumped
clean out of the way.

Prince Freddie raced over the drawbridge
and crashed through the castle gates.

The dragon was super impressed. No one had **ever** stood up to her before.
It was surprising and interesting and . . .

"**Fantastic!**" she roared
and accidentally set fire to the castle!

"**Oops,**" said the dragon.

"**Oh no!**" said Sir Rushington.

But Prince Freddie said . . .

"At last!"

And suddenly there was an almighty sizzle.

The fire was completely put out and Castle Crumbly was saved.

"**Righty-ho!**" said Prince Freddie.
"Back to my holiday!"

"Your master is the bravest of the brave,"
said the dragon to Sir Rushington.
"Do let me give your noble prince a lift."

"It would be an honour,"
said Sir Rushington.

So off they flew, over the mountains. They hadn't gone very far when Sir Rushington said, "Madam, could we stop, please?"

"Why?" asked the dragon.

Sir Rushington blushed. "I need a poo!"

First published 2017 by Nosy Crow Ltd
The Crow's Nest, Baden Place, Crosby Row
London SE1 1YW
www.nosycrow.com

ISBN 978 0 85763 821 2 (HB)
ISBN 978 0 85763 825 0 (PB)

Nosy Crow and associated logos are trademarks
and/or registered trademarks of Nosy Crow Ltd.

Text © Greg Gormley 2017
Illustrations © Chris Mould 2017
The right of Greg Gormley to be identified as
the author of this work and of Chris Mould to be
identified as the illustrator of this work has been asserted.

A CIP catalogue record for this book is available from the British Library.

Printed in Turkey by Imago.
Papers used by Nosy Crow are made from wood grown in sustainable forests.

10 9 8 7 6 5 4 3 2 1 (HB)
10 9 8 7 6 5 4 3 2 1 (PB)

For Roxana and Fran
G. G.

If you needed to go before you sat down to read
this story, this book is dedicated to you
C. M.